Sam the School Pony

That afternoon, after lessons, Becky went to the field as usual.

"Hey, Sam!" she called.

But Sam didn't trot over to the gate to meet her like he usually did. He stood over by the fence, panting. He looked ill. What was wrong?

All of Jenny Dale's PONY TALES™ books can
be ordered at your local bookshop or are
available by post from Bookpost
(tel: 01624 836000)

Sam the School Pony

by Jenny Dale

Illustrated by Frank Rodgers

A Working Partners Book

MACMILLAN CHILDREN'S BOOKS

Special thanks to Ann Ruffell

First published 2000 by Macmillan Children's Books
a division of Pan Macmillan Ltd
20 New Wharf Road, London N1 9RR
Basingstoke and Oxford
www.panmacmillan.com

Associated companies throughout the world

Created by Working Partners Limited
London W6 0QT

ISBN 0 330 37468 0

13 15 17 19 18 16 14

A CIP catalogue record for this book is available from
the British Library.

Typeset by SX Composing DTP, Rayleigh, Essex
Printed by Mackays of Chatham plc, Kent

Chapter One

"Hey, Sam! Look what I've brought you!" Becky Brown called. She scrambled over the gate and dropped down into the muddy field on the other side.

The little pony who lived in the field trotted over to Becky. "So you're here at last!" he whinnied. "I thought you'd forgotten."

Usually Becky got to Sam's field very early in the morning, before all the other children even thought of leaving for school. She always had something special for the pony to eat – a crunchy carrot or a crisp apple. She was so early that there was always plenty of time to play with him before school started.

Becky ran up to Sam and gave him a hug. "I'm sorry I'm late," she said. "I dropped cereal on my school shirt and Mum made me change it."

Sam nuzzled at the school bag. He could smell something delicious in there.

"You know just where I've put your snack, don't you?" laughed Becky. She took the bag off her shoulder and opened it.

Sam shoved his muzzle into the bag and rummaged about in between books and pencils until he found what he wanted. "Ah! That's what I'm looking for," he whinnied. "A big juicy carrot. Ooh, great – there's an apple here too!"

He munched the carrot, dribbling orange-coloured juice.

"Be careful!" scolded Becky. "I'll get into real trouble if my shirt gets dirty again." She stroked the pony's muzzle.

He whickered, "I love being scratched on my nose!"

"Who do you belong to?" asked Becky thoughtfully. "I've seen your owner ride you sometimes. I wonder if she comes over again when we've gone home from school."

Sam threw up his head and neighed. "Of course she does." He turned and trotted round in a circle, just to show off.

Becky laughed. "And does she take you to gymkhanas and canter with you over the fields?"

Sam blew down his nose. "I've done it all," he whickered to Becky.

The pony had arrived at the field next to the school two weeks ago. In a corner was a new shelter and over the top was a sign saying 'SAM'.

Quite near the gate was a tub full of water. Some days when Becky was looking out of her classroom window she saw an old Land Rover drive up to the field. A tall lady jumped out and filled the trough with water from a large can. Becky watched Sam try to snatch mouthfuls of hay from the bales the lady carried to the shelter. Sometimes a girl came in the Land Rover too. They put a saddle and bridle on the pony, and the girl rode him around the field.

Sam nudged Becky to see if she had anything else to eat.

"I wish you were mine," said Becky wistfully, "even though you're so cheeky. I've always wanted a pony, but Mum says we haven't got enough money."

She gave Sam another pat. "Come on. Let's play."

She pretended she was on a pony and trotted round in a circle, as if she was in the arena of a riding school. Then she turned, and trotted the other way. She sloshed through the wet field, mud spattering the backs of her legs.

Sam followed her. This was a good game! Then he decided to canter to the other side of the field and back, just to show Becky that he could go fast if he wanted to.

Suddenly Sam wheeled around and cantered back to the gate.

Becky looked round. Perhaps it was the tall lady, coming to fill up the pony's water trough.

But it was someone else – the girl Becky had seen from the school window. She looked a bit older than Becky. She was wearing jodphurs and a riding hat. Sam was nuzzling her hand.

Becky ran over to the gate. "Is he your pony?" she asked. "He's so lovely!" Suddenly Becky felt very shy. Perhaps the girl wouldn't like her being in the field with Sam. "Oh, I'm sorry, I hope you don't mind me being here," she added quickly.

"I don't mind," said the girl. "Sam loves to be with people. He's been friendly since he was a foal."

"Thank you. I love coming to see him," smiled Becky.

"I'm Joanne Bates, by the way," said the girl. "What's your name?"

"Becky. Becky Brown," replied Becky. "Are you new here?"

"We've just moved," said Joanne. Then she stopped.

Sam whickered softly. Becky looked up and saw huge tears rolling down the girl's face.

"What's the matter?" Becky blurted out.

Joanne rubbed her eyes. "I'm going away to boarding school tomorrow," she sniffed.

"I'm sorry," said Becky. How awful it would be to have to leave home to go to school.

"Oh, I don't mind about school," said Joanne. "Lots of my friends will be there too."

"So what's the matter?" asked Becky.

"It's Sam," explained Joanne. She threw her arms around the pony's neck and hugged him. "I love him to bits, but I can't take him to school and he's going to be so miserable." She gulped a little then went on. "But that's not the worst thing. By the time I get back at Christmas I'll be too big for him. I've grown a bit over the summer already. I won't be able to ride him any more. Mum says we might have to sell him!"

Chapter Two

At dinner break Becky told her
friends all about Joanne and Sam.

There was a gate between Sam's
field and the school playing field.
The children sat on it and watched
Sam show off.

"What a shame Joanne's got to
lose her pony just because she's

getting too big," said Julie Grey.

"If they sell him we won't have a pony next to our school any more," said Tom Dymond.

"Let's kidnap him!" cried Julie.

"Where could we take him?" asked Becky. "There isn't room in my garden."

"Join a circus!" said Gary Taylor. "We can all go with him and be acrobats." Gary liked swinging upside down on the wall bars at school.

But there wasn't a circus anywhere nearby.

"Take him to the horse sanctuary," suggested Tom.

"That's daft!" said Julie. "Sanctuaries only take horses and ponies that are hurt or not wanted. Anybody can see that Sam is very well looked after!"

Sam cantered over for a pat. He nuzzled at Becky, and she rubbed his nose. "Mmm – that feels good!" he whinnied. "Are there any carrots around, or even a very small apple?" Swishing his tail, he moved along the fence so that Tom could reach his neck. "Or how about a crunchy peppermint? I can smell peppermints. I know one of you has got some!"

Sam nosed at Tom's pocket, curious to know what was inside, but there was only the smell of peppermints left.

Julie ran to the corner of the playing field where there was some juicy grass. She pulled up a

handful and ran back to Sam.
"Here, Sam. Have some of this."

Sam snorted. "I've had rather a lot of that already. But thank you anyway."

Tom had some salad in his sandwich box. He didn't like salad very much. He hoped Sam might.

"Interesting!" blew Sam. He took the salad delicately from Tom's hand and accidentally left green dribble on his arm.

It was a beautiful autumn day, and Sam felt very frisky. "Why don't you all have a ride?" he whinnied. "I like people riding me. It's good fun!"

He circled round and galloped off to show what good fun it could be.

"Bye, Sam, I've got some painting to finish," said Julie, climbing over the gate again. "I'm going back to school."

"Me too," said Tom. "Come on, Gary, we're supposed to be playing football."

But Becky stayed with Sam. There wasn't anything else she would rather do.

Sam came back to keep her company, leaping over some grassy tussocks on the way.

"They ought to put up some jumps for you," said Becky. She scratched him in just the right place on his nose. "You're really good at jumping."

"Thanks," whinnied Sam. "But right now I need a good roll. I'll come back soon."

"Don't go away, Sam!" cried Becky. But the pony trotted off to a nice flat part of his field, lay down and rolled from side to side.

"You look as if you're really enjoying that!" Becky called. While she was waiting for him to come back, she thought hard. Poor Joanne! It would be awful if Sam

was sold. Especially if he was sold
to someone who wouldn't love
him as much as Joanne did.

Sam suddenly stopped rolling
and stood up. He gave a loud
whinny and cantered across the
field.

But he wasn't going to see Becky
this time. He made for the gate
that opened onto the lane.

"Hello, Sam!" It was the lady Becky had seen before. She had come in her Land Rover to feed Sam. Becky realised the woman must be Joanne's mum, Mrs Bates.

She went over to say hello.

Sam pushed his head over the fence and nuzzled at Mrs Bates's pocket.

"You're so greedy!" said Mrs Bates, laughing. "You know just where to find your treats, don't you?"

"He can find them at the bottom of my school bag as well," Becky agreed. "I bring him something every day." And then she stopped. "Is that all right?" she asked.

"I'm sure Sam loves it," said Mrs

Bates. "He's going to miss Joanne riding him. Are you Becky? She told me about you."

"Yes, I am – couldn't you ride him?" suggested Becky, without thinking.

Mrs Bates laughed. "Me? I'm far too big. Even Joanne's getting too tall for him now. I'm afraid we might have to sell him. The trouble is, he's so much a part of the family we'd all miss him, but it's not fair to leave him here without any company and nobody to ride him."

Becky's heart was pounding. She'd had a brilliant idea. Dare she tell Mrs Bates what it was?

Her mouth opened and shut like a goldfish's.

"I – I—" she began, but she just couldn't get it out.

Then Sam decided to butt in. He leaned his head over Becky's shoulder and nuzzled her ear with his soft mouth. "Why don't you ride me?" he whickered.

"Do you think?" began Becky. She stopped. She didn't know

how to ask.

"Go on," whinnied Sam.

"What are you trying to say, Becky?" said Mrs Bates.

"Well, I just thought," Becky mumbled, "that if Sam needs company and someone to ride him, why couldn't we help? I mean, my class. We're all friendly with Sam. We're doing an Animal Care project and this would be perfect. We could feed him and groom him as well."

Sam pricked up his ears. That sounded like a great idea! Becky's class was very nice, and Becky would groom him really thoroughly.

"Well," said Mrs Bates slowly, "it would certainly help me. And I suppose if you can all ride . . ."

Becky's mouth dropped open. How completely stupid. She hadn't even thought about *that*!

As far as she knew, absolutely *nobody* in her class knew how to ride a pony!

Chapter Three

Sam was so excited that he
decided to show off a little.
He pawed the ground and
blew down his nostrils, then
trotted sideways for a few paces
before rearing and neighing
loudly.

"N – no," said Becky, looking at

Sam. "I don't think any of us knows how to ride."

"Hmm," frowned Mrs Bates. "Sam might be a bit too frisky for beginners."

Bother! thought Sam. *I shouldn't have done that. Better stand still and show them how safe I am.*

He ambled back to the fence and stood looking out into the lane.

Becky scratched him behind the ears. She wanted to throw her arms around his neck and cuddle him. But her stomach was tight with disappointment. She shouldn't even have thought of riding Sam! It only made things worse.

"Is that your school bell ringing?" said Mrs Bates

suddenly. "Don't be late back for afternoon lessons."

Becky could hear everyone running in. She gave Sam a last pat on his neck and began to walk slowly back to the gate into the school playing field.

"By the way, what's the name of your head teacher?" called Mrs Bates as Becky reached the gate. "Joanne and I might go and have a word with him this afternoon, when she's finished her packing."

Two days later Mr Duncan, the head teacher, came into Miss Jones's class with Mrs Bates.

Becky clenched her fists under the table.

Mr Duncan introduced Mrs Bates, and then he smiled at them all.

"I had a word with Miss Jones, and we think it will be a very good idea for the class to help Mrs Bates by grooming Sam and assisting with his general care," he said. "You will be able to write all about it for your Animal Care project."

Everyone cheered and banged on their tables.

Becky held her breath. She would do anything for Sam, but she desperately wanted to be able to ride him too.

"And Mrs Bates has agreed to come in twice a week at dinner break and give riding lessons to

all those people who want them,"
added Miss Jones.

Becky let her breath out.
"Wow!"

As soon as the bell went,
everyone raced to the field with
Mrs Bates.

"There's another job you can

help with as well," said Mrs Bates. "See that tall yellow weed behind the taped-off section?"

Everyone looked over to where she pointed. There were thick pieces of white tape across the corner of the field like a fence, and some bright yellow flowers a long way behind it.

"That's called ragwort. I've managed to clear most of it. There's only that corner left. If you're not riding you could help to dig up the rest of it. Then Sam can have the whole of his field to play in."

Mrs Bates came over every day for the first week to tell them what to do.

"I'll go and get Sam!" said Becky on the second day. She was first to get changed into her trousers and sweater. She rushed off to the field carrying Sam's head collar.

"Hey, Sam!" she called. "Time for our lessons!"

"Lessons?" snorted Sam. "Who needs lessons? But I'd love an apple," he whickered, nudging Becky's arm.

"Sorry, I haven't any apples today," said Becky. "Here's your carrot."

Sam bent his head to take the carrot from Becky's palm. But just as Becky went to put the halter rope around his neck, Sam pulled his head back and pranced off to the other side of the field.

"Come here, Sam!" shouted Becky, running after him. She skidded on a damp patch and fell on her bottom. "Oh, Sam, please come back!" she yelled, getting up. "Don't you want us to learn how to look after you?"

Sam trotted back and nosed at her hand. "Don't be silly, of course I do," he blew. "I was just feeling excited, that's all."

Mrs Bates was at the gate, wearing a wide-brimmed leather hat. She waved at Becky.

"Don't stand any nonsense from him," she said. "Let him know who's boss. Come on, Sam. Bring Becky with you."

Sam led Becky through the gate into the school playing field. She tied him to the fence with the rope attached to his head collar. The children crowded round. They all wanted to groom him.

It looks as if I'm going to have a good time here, thought Sam. He snuffled at Tom's tracksuit top. There was a picture of a pony on it.

Tom laughed. "Stop tickling, Sam," he said. "Do you think the picture looks like you?"

But Sam wasn't listening. He was too busy being petted by Becky and her friends to pay attention to Tom.

Chapter Four

There seemed a lot of things to know about before Becky and her classmates could ride Sam. They learned to brush the mud from his legs, dig out the stones from his hooves and comb his mane. They found out that he loved peppermints for a treat.

At last, at the beginning of the second week, Mrs Bates said they could have riding lessons.

First they had to put on Sam's bridle. Gary had the first go. He dropped the reins over the pony's neck. Then he tried to get the bit – a shiny metal bar – into Sam's mouth at the same time as lifting the bridle's leather headpiece over the pony's ears. It all seemed very difficult!

"Oops!" blew Sam, yanking his head backwards. "Hold on a minute."

"Just let him open his mouth for you," said Mrs Bates.

"It's only because I wasn't ready," whickered Sam. He opened his mouth properly and

Gary pushed the bit comfortably behind his teeth.

"You use the reins and your legs to direct him," said Mrs Bates. "It sounds difficult, but you'll soon get the hang of it."

Then the children had to put the saddle on. Sam stood completely still while they tightened the girth around his tummy.

"You'll deserve two peppermints after this," whispered Becky.

"How about the whole packet?" neighed Sam hopefully. He bent his head and shook the bridle until it jingled.

At last all Sam's tack was on. He was really looking forward to a good ride. He threw up his head and neighed. "Come on, then. Are you first, Becky?"

"Stand still, Sam," said Mrs Bates. She was making sure the stirrup was long enough to enable Becky to mount.

"Please, Sam," said Becky. "We won't be long now. It's just that we don't know how to do things and we've got to learn." She patted his neck. "And then you can have your peppermint."

Mrs Bates showed Becky how to fit her boot into the stirrup and pull herself up into the saddle. She thought it was funny to have to start by facing the pony's tail!

All the time Sam stood stock-still, but he was beginning to feel a little bored. He shook his head and pawed the ground gently to attract Mrs Bates's attention.

"Can't we do something interesting now?" he snorted as Becky settled herself in the saddle and Mrs Bates checked the stirrups. "Can I start walking?"

Mrs Bates patted his neck. "Well done, Sam. You've been very patient. Now, Becky, tap with your heels so that Sam will know you want him to walk."

Becky nudged him with her heels, and Sam walked on, with Mrs Bates holding a leading rein attached to Sam's bridle.

"Doesn't it hurt him if I tap his sides?" asked Becky.

Sam turned his head and whickered, "No, you're very gentle. Great! We're on the move at last!"

Becky felt fantastic up there on Sam's back. She held the reins in just the way Mrs Bates had showed her. Then she eased her right leg into Sam's side and gently felt the right rein – and Sam started bending to the right. Becky was thrilled! Sam knew exactly what she wanted to do.

"Well done," snorted Sam. "You're a natural!"

All too soon though Becky had to get off and let someone else have a turn.

In the end only a few of the class decided that they wanted to ride. Tom and Gary preferred football. Julie liked to groom Sam but she was a bit frightened when he was a little frisky. She preferred to dig up the ragwort from the field.

Becky was the first to ride on her own, without the leading rein. Soon she began to learn to trot and canter. But there were still six people who wanted lessons, and even with Mrs Bates coming along twice a week it seemed such a long time before it was her turn.

"One lesson every two weeks isn't nearly enough," Becky told Sam before school one day. Today it was her turn to collect manure in the school wheelbarrow instead of having a lesson. That was OK, but not as much fun as sitting on Sam's back and imagining herself as a champion rider.

"Why don't you stay on after school and ride me then?" he whinnied. "We could have a lot of fun together. You're doing really well and I love it when you come to visit me."

"Oh, well, it's great I can ride you a little," sighed Becky. "Anyway, even if I'll never be able to take you for a proper ride at least I can stay after school to talk to you."

That afternoon, after lessons, Becky went to the field as usual. "Hey, Sam!" she called.

But Sam didn't trot over to the gate to meet her like he usually did. He stood over by the white tape fence, panting. He looked ill. What was wrong?

Chapter Five

"Sam – Sam – what's the matter?" said Becky anxiously. She raced over to him. His eyes were dull and he didn't seem to want to move.

"You were all right at dinner break," she said, stroking his neck. "What's happened since then?"

Sam snuffled pathetically. "It hurts here," he whickered as he tried to turn his head to rub his belly.

Becky ran her hand over his tummy. Sam shrank back slightly.

"Oh, Sam, you poor thing." Becky hugged him, but he could barely raise his head.

Suddenly she remembered something. She had been reading about ragwort in a book she found in the school library. It was terribly poisonous to ponies. That was why Mrs Bates had got the children to clear the field of the yellow plants. There was only a tiny bit left now.

"Have you broken through the fence?" Becky looked anxiously at

the white tape. It seemed to be in the same place as it always had been. When Becky's classmates dug out ragwort they crawled underneath the tape to get at it. The remains of the weed were much too far away for Sam to reach.

Then Becky saw a heap of ragwort stems by the gate, mixed up with some hay. Someone must have pulled them out and left them there by mistake. And Sam had nibbled the dangerous weed!

Becky's heart went thump, right down into her shoes.

"I'm going for help, Sam," she said breathlessly, running for the gate.

*

Miss Jones was just about to leave the school. She had her coat on and was carrying a bag of books for marking.

"Hello, Becky. Have you forgotten something?" the teacher asked.

"It's Sam," babbled Becky. "We've got to call the vet!"

"Tell me what's happened, Becky," said Miss Jones. She put her bag down.

"We've got to be quick!" cried Becky. "He's been poisoned!"

"Are you sure?" said Miss Jones. "Perhaps we'd better call Mrs Bates first." She turned back to the school office.

"No! No!" said Becky. "We must call the vet first. He might die if we wait!"

Miss Jones seemed to take hours finding the vet's number in the phone directory. But at last she got through and explained quickly what had happened.

"Here," she said, handing Becky the phone. "The vet wants to know Sam's symptoms."

Becky grabbed the receiver. The vet asked so many questions. Why didn't he just come! Somehow Becky managed to explain how Sam looked, and about the dried ragwort by the gate. The vet said he would come straight away.

Becky raced back to the field while Miss Jones telephoned Mrs Bates.

The vet seemed to take hours to

arrive! And all the time poor Sam panted and trembled. Becky stroked him. "Help will be here soon, Sam," she whispered. "Just hold on!"

Eventually Becky heard a car coming along the lane. It was the vet at last! And Mrs Bates's Land Rover was right behind him.

Becky ran to meet them at the gate. Mrs Bates looked very worried.

"Will he be all right?" sobbed Becky.

Mrs Bates held Becky's hand while the vet looked Sam over. Then he opened his bag. "Hold the pony's head while I give him an injection," he told Becky.

"It's all right, Sam," whispered

Becky. "The vet's going to make you better." But Sam was feeling too poorly to even look at her.

When the vet had finished, he turned to Mrs Bates. "Keep him quiet for a week or so," he said. "No riding, of course! I'll pop over again tomorrow, but I think we got here just in time."

*

When Becky's friends heard about Sam the next morning they were shocked.

Tom shivered. "How can he be so ill just from eating a weed?" he said.

Julie felt really bad. She was the one who had left the plants by the gate. She had meant to take them to the bonfire site, but the school bell had rung so she left them on the ground to collect later.

Mrs Bates said it wasn't Julie's fault. "I should have told you how important it was to clear the stuff away immediately," she said. "But the vet has seen Sam again this morning and says he will be properly better in a couple of weeks."

"We'll have a special work party in the field this week," said Mr Duncan. "Nobody can ride until Sam is properly better, so that gives us a chance to get rid of the last bits of ragwort."

"And it's all thanks to Becky that he's already so much better," said Mrs Bates, smiling. "She guessed what was wrong and acted very fast."

Becky grinned. "It was lucky I'd just been reading about it," she said.

"It's more than that," said Mrs Bates. "You really care about Sam."

Becky visited Sam in his field every day. Mrs Bates gave her

Joanne's address at her boarding school so that Becky could write and tell her how much better he looked. Joanne wrote back to ask about Sam and to say thank you to Becky for looking after him.

Then, one morning, Mrs Bates telephoned Becky to tell her that Sam was well enough to start their riding lessons again.

"And I've got a special surprise for you," she added. "I'll meet you at the gate in ten minutes."

Becky ran to the field as soon as she had finished her breakfast. What was the special news?

Sam came cantering over to the gate, just as if he'd never been ill at all.

"Where have you been?" he

whinnied. "I've been looking out for you for ages!" He nosed into Becky's school bag to see if there were any goodies for him.

"Wait a minute!" cried Becky. "Let me find your carrot."

But Sam had already found it and was crunching happily.

Becky laughed. "You look better than ever," she said. "You're going to be a handful when we start our lessons again."

She scratched him on his nose in just the way he liked.

"Something special's going to happen today. I can feel it!" whickered Sam, nuzzling her hand with his soft mouth.

Becky felt very excited when Mrs Bates drove up the lane. She

and Sam went to meet her.
"What's the surprise?" asked
Becky. "Is Joanne going to get
another pony?"

Mrs Bates smiled. "Yes, but
that's not the real surprise," she
said. "Joanne and I have had a
great idea. If your mum says it's
all right, I'm going to give you
extra riding lessons after school."

Becky was speechless with delight.

"What did I tell you?" Sam neighed. "I knew it was going to be a great day!"

"When Joanne comes home from school at Christmas we'll choose a new pony for her," said Mrs Bates. "With a few extra lessons you'll be able to go out riding with them on Sam. What do you think?"

Sam threw up his head and shook his mane. "Fantastic!" he neighed.

"But – will I be good enough to ride with her by then?" Becky cried.

Sam snorted. "You'll be really brilliant," he said.

"Of course you will. You've been

my best pupil," laughed Mrs Bates. "And you can come and help look after Sam whenever you like."

Even though Sam still belonged to Joanne, Becky felt as if all her dreams had come true.

"What could be more perfect?" whinnied Sam. "Becky and Joanne – my two best friends!"

Collect all of JENNY DALE'S PONY TALES™!

The prices shown below are correct at the time of going to press.
However, Macmillan Publishers reserves the right to show new retail
prices on covers which may differ from those previously advertised.

JENNY DALE'S PONY TALES™

Sam the School Pony	0 330 37468 0	£2.99
Charlie the Champion Pony	0 330 37469 9	£3.99
Lottie the Little Pony	0 330 37472 9	£2.99
Shadow the Secret Pony	0 330 37474 5	£2.99
Rosie the Runaway Pony	0 330 37473 7	£3.50
Willow the Wild Pony	0 330 37475 3	£2.99

All Pan Macmillan titles can be ordered from our website,
www.panmacmillan.com, or your local bookshop
and are also available by post from:

**Bookpost
PO Box 29, Douglas, Isle of Man IM99 1BQ**

Credit cards accepted. For details:
Telephone: 01624 677237
Fax: 01624 670923
E-mail: bookshop@enterprise.net
www.bookpost.co.uk

Free postage and packing in the United Kingdom